Father Christmas's puzzle

Which way did Father Christmas go to deliver the presents?

Christmas lights

Colour the light that comes next in each row to complete the pattern.

Let's go to a pantomime

Draw a line to join each pair of pantomime characters.
Colour the blank pictures.

Old King Cole

Which crown is the king wearing?
Colour the picture.

Christmas presents

Who got which present?

Snowflakes

Which snowflake is the odd one out?

Christmas counting

Look at the picture and write the answers to the questions in the boxes.

How many...

mice ☐

owls ☐

houses ☐

stars ☐

windows ☐

Santas ☐

Christmas stockings

Unscramble the letters to find out what was in each stocking.

Match each stocking with the correct picture.

Christmas clown

Colour the balloons using the key.

r –   b –

g –   y –

Christmas picture crossword

Use the pictures to help you to fill in the crossword.

Across

Down

A Christmas crib

Colour this Nativity scene.

How many Christmas objects?

Draw a line to join the numeral to the correct number of items.

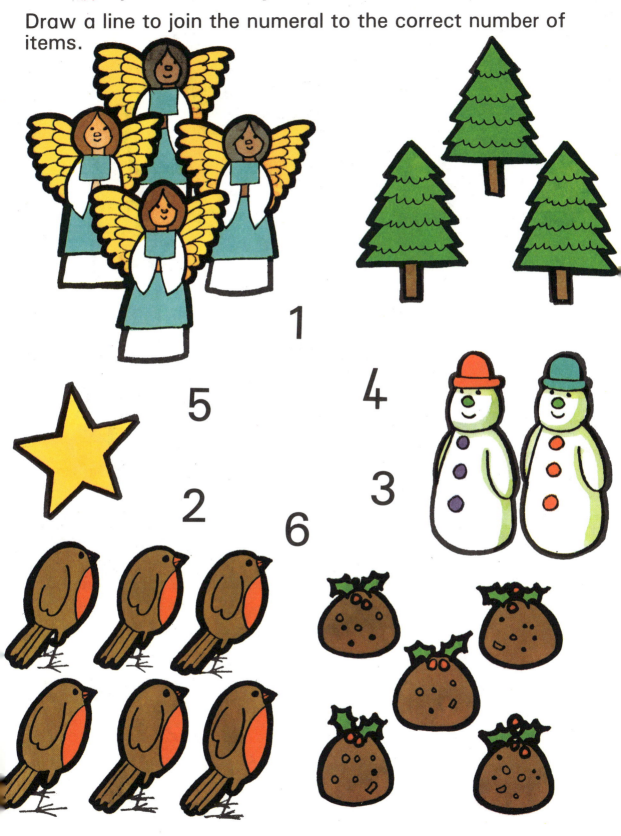

1

5

4

2

3

6

Circus time

Join up the dots to see what the clowns are doing.

Christmas cake

Choose some decorations from those below to draw on the cake. Colour your picture.

A letter to Father Christmas

Find the pairs

Which two are the same in each row?

Christmas crackers

Match the halves of each cracker.

Nursery rhymes

Match the nursery rhyme characters to their Christmas presents.

Father Christmas down the chimney

Spot 6 differences in the bottom picture.

Christmas bells

Count the bells in this jumbled picture.
Which is the odd one out?

Party hats

Find another one

like this...

like this...

like this...

like this...

like this...

Rudolph the red-nose reindeer

One reindeer is different from the others.
Can you find him?

Christmas I-spy

Find at least ten things in the picture that begin with the letter **c**.

Christmas candles

Draw the correct number of candles on each domino.

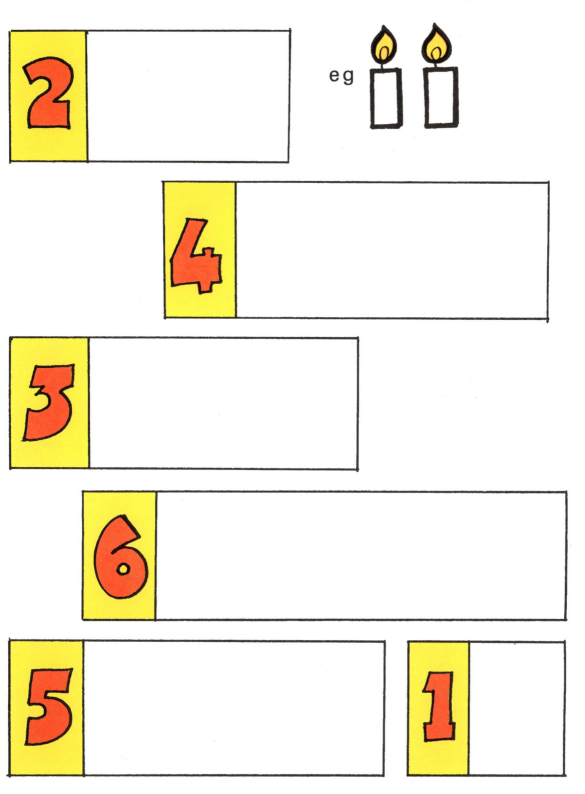

eg

There are four presents hanging on the tree

Join the dots to find out what they are, then colour the picture.